Ten in the Meadow

For Finn Eric
J. B.

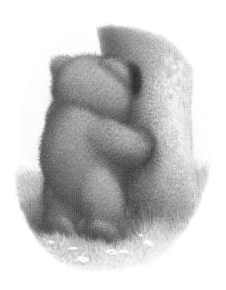

Published by
PEACHTREE PUBLISHERS
1700 Chattahoochee Avenue
Atlanta, Georgia 30318-2112
www.peachtree-online.com

ISBN 1-56145-372-2

First published in Great Britain in 2005 by Orchard Books.

Printed in Singapore
10 9 8 7 6 5 4 3 2 1
First edition

Illustrations created in acrylics and colored pencil.

www.johnbutlerart.com

Library of Congress Cataloging-in-Publication Data

Butler, John, 1952-
  Ten in the meadow / by John Butler.-- 1st ed.
    p. cm.
  Summary: As a group of forest animals plays a lively game of hide-and-
seek in a meadow, Bear finds them each in turn--except the elusive
Mousey.
  ISBN 1-56145-372-2 (alk. paper)
 [1. Hide-and-seek--Fiction. 2. Forest animals--Fiction.] I. Title.
  PZ8.3.B9788Ten 2006
  [E]--dc22
                                                    2005037702

Ten in the Meadow

John Butler

PEACHTREE
ATLANTA

Round and round the meadow,
Running here and there.
Ten little friends play hide-and-seek!

"Quickly, hide from Bear!"

Round and
round the daisies,
Bear shouts, "Here I come!"

He's searching . . .

he's looking . . .

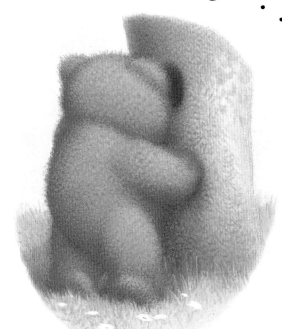

Here, he's found someone!

Round and round the foxgloves,

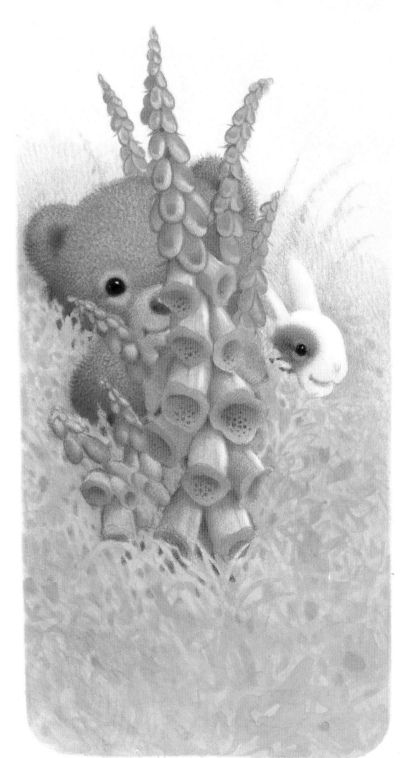

The two friends take a look.

Among the flowers, under leaves,

They peek in every nook.

"Found you, Porcupine!"

"Found you, Mole!"

Round and
round the bluebells,
The friends join in the race.

Looking here . . .

looking there . . .

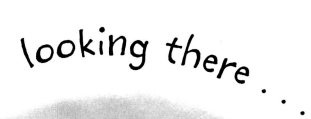

They've found a hiding place!

Round and round
the old oak,

Now what can
they see?

Little paws and
bushy tails . . .

Who is up
the tree?

"Found you, Squirrel!"
"Found you, Raccoon!"

Who's that under the lily pads?
Shall we take a look?

Round and round the rushes,
By the trickling brook.

Round and round the clover,
The sun is sinking low.
Rabbit says, "Now, where is Mouse?
Does anybody know?"

"Where are you, Mouse?"

Round and round
the willow,

Where can
Mousey be?

Bear says,
"I think I know...

Quickly, follow me!"

Back home from the meadow,
The friends all take a peep.
Curled up snugly in the den,
Mouse lies fast asleep!

"Shh, sleepy-time, everyone . . . "

Ten friends asleep together,
Below the crescent moon.
They dream about tomorrow's fun,
And games they'll all play soon.

Good night! Sleep tight!